£2.00

D1549924

EVERY CAT
IN THE BOOK

EVERY CAT IN THE BOOK

Written and illustrated by,

Willie Rushton

PAVILION

First published in Great Britain in 1993
PAVILION BOOKS LIMITED
26 Upper Ground, London SE1 9PD

Copyright © 1993 Willie Rushton

ANDY CATT

All rights reserved. No part of this publication may be reproduced, stored in
a retrieval system, or transmitted, in any form or by any means, electronic,
mechanical, photocopying, recording or otherwise, without the prior permission
of the copyright holders.

A CIP catalogue record for this book is available from the British Library

ISBN 1 85793 199 8

Printed and bound in the UK

2 4 6 8 10 9 7 5 3 1

This book may be ordered by post direct from the publisher.
Please contact the
Marketing Department. But try your bookshop first.

FOREWORD

MEATBALL

This book has been lurking in the dark corridors of my bosom for a good number of years now. I drew a very rough version of the A's about ten years ago as a birthday card or such for Afro-American Actress and Artiste, Alibe Parsons, (you can see why), though to tell the truth she's more into bears. Ten years later I stole them back off her, and continued from B to Z. I felt it was time I paid my homage to cats.

Now the reason I have always preferred cats to dogs (and I've enjoyed both) is that while dogs are Drama Queens — the doleful eyes, the heavy breathing — cats are essentially comedians. It's the fact that they look so serious that makes their every movement, or lack of it, funny. You could put on a production of Hamlet with dogs. Lassie would make a breathless Gertrude. Rin Tin Tin, I see as Claudius. Snoopy, perhaps, as the Prince of Denmark. You wouldn't catch our cat in it. Oh all right, 2nd Gravedigger then.

I've known a few cats in my time. The first I remember was down in Wales, to which I moved for World War II. A number of them were named after Russian Generals — Tamashenkov was one, or something very similar, and of course there was a Winston. Winston begged like a dog which dog-lovers thought clever, but cat-persons viewed as cheap. Back to London and a long-lived cat called Gus after Gustavus Adolphus, the Lion of the North. My mother insisted that he was Persian. He was pure Alley. The best ones are.

Since then there has been Bonjour, named by my son Toby as a tribute to the French cousine who gave her to him. Bonjour was magnificent and we often suspected a reincarnation of Joan Crawford. Then came Meatball rescued from the dustbins of Earls Court by a florist and still with us. The Third Cat was Orson who looked like Louis the Fourteenth and behaved almost as badly. I dedicate this book to them all, particularly to Meatball who, as I said, is still with us and wonderfully funny. Thanks, cats.

BERTRAND is Cat at the Grand Hotel
And keeps a firm eye on the Clientelle
The Hotel's at its' busiest most afternoons
Bertrand purrs at the ladies and counts the spoons.

CATS ARE MOST CONTENTED
CREATURES - RARELY SUICIDAL
ADMITTEDLY THEY LIVE NINE LIVES
BUT ALL OF THEM ARE IDLE.

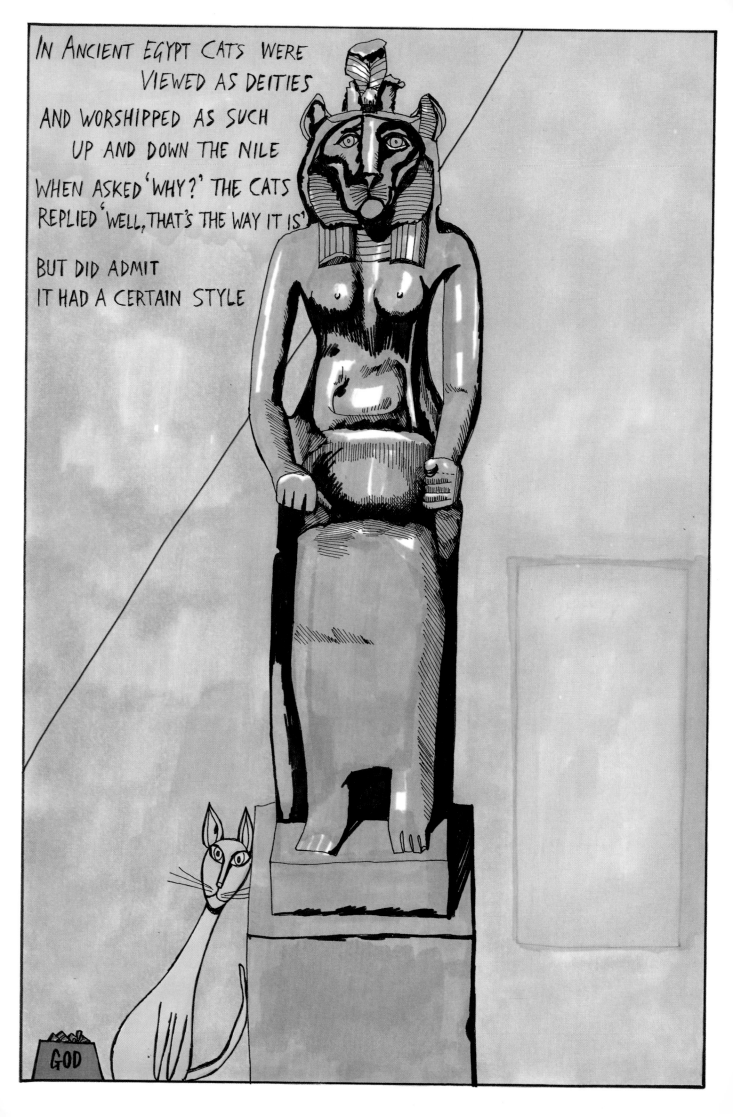

This Cat Belongs to Sigmund Freud
And is not exactly over-joyed
Should he piss in Sigmund's Nike
The old fool starts to probe his psyche.

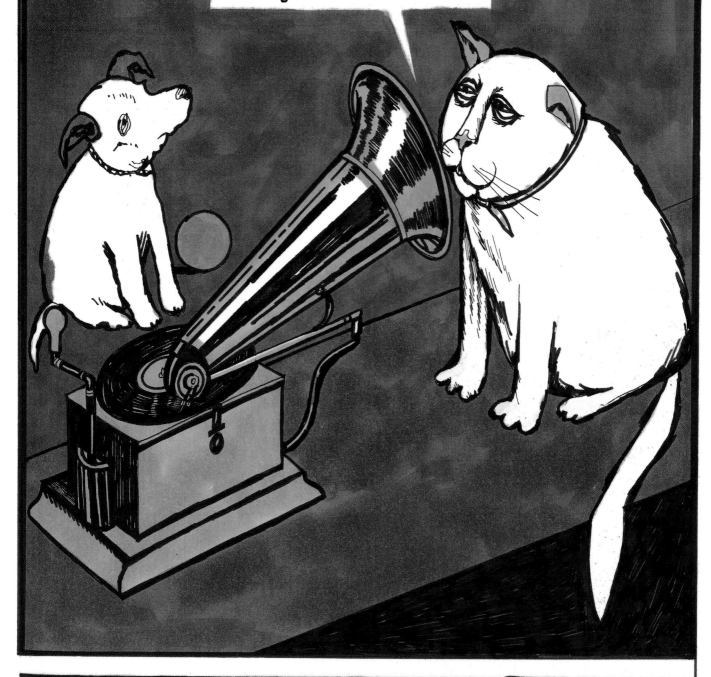

IF YOU SAY 'SIT!' TO A DOG, THE DOG'S AS GOOD AS SAT —

I'D LIKE TO SEE YOU TRY THAT WITH A CAT.

There once was an Edward called LEAR
Who many suggest was quite queer
If it's queer to cavort
With your cat, I'd have thought
I, for one, was as queer as old Lear

LABOUR CAT

The LEANING CAT of PISA

THE L-SHAPED CAT

LEGIONNAIRE'S CAT

THE LAUGHING CAT

LOURDES CAT

CLEAN

LORD'S CAT

LAST OF THE MOHICATS

LATERAL THINKING CAT

LORD LUCAN'S CAT

LUVVY CATS

KEN

EM

The MAGNIFICENT SEVEN CATS

MANX CAT

MAGRITTE'S CAT

Marcel Duchamp's Cat.

MAMMOTH CAT

MEDIUM CAT

MINIMAL CAT

MILLS & BOON CAT

MONTGOLFIER'S CAT

MADAME TUSSAUD'S CAT

MEXICAN CAT DANCE

MOSES' CAT

THE ONE COMMANDMENT
1. THOU SHALT NOT FORGET TO FEED THE CAT
GOD

MIDSUMMER NIGHT'S CAT

MONARCH OF THE GLEN CAT

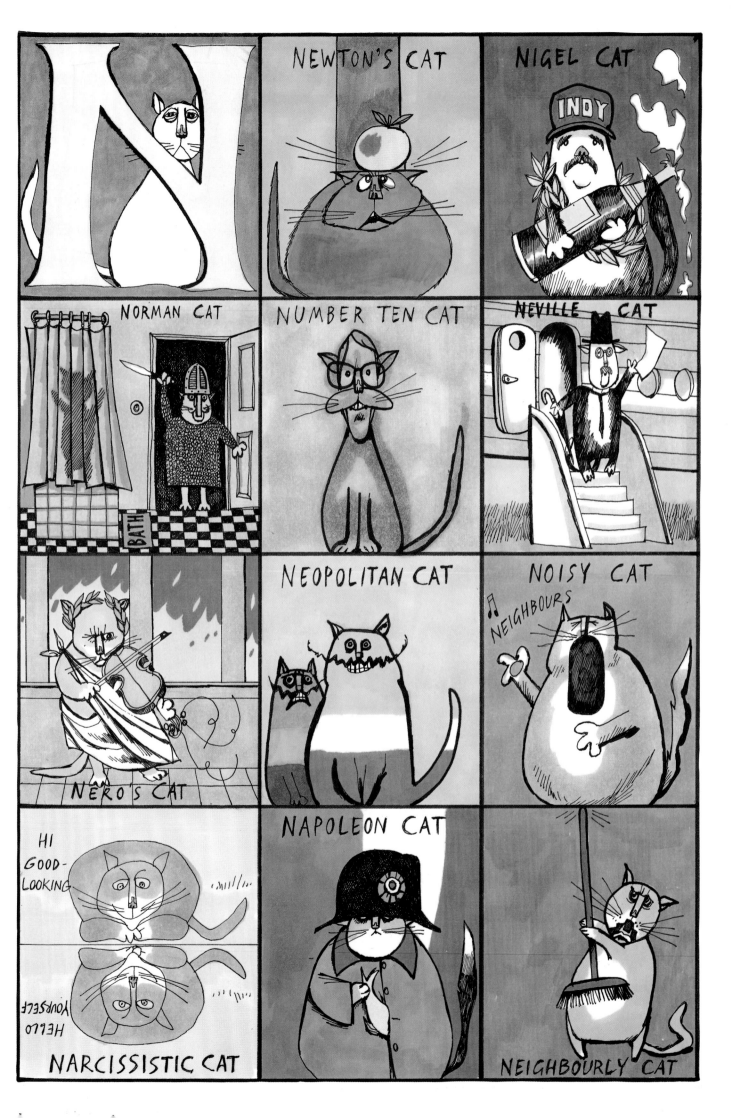

CITIZEN KAT

THE THIRD CAT

ORSON CAT

OWL-LIKE CAT

OSTRICH-LIKE CAT

OVOID CAT

OSCAR CAT

CAT OSCAR

FELIX
BEST ACTOR

ONAN the BARBARIAN CAT

ORVILLE CAT

OLYMPIC CAT

ORANGE CAT

The OLD CURIOSITY CAT

CURIOSITY KILLING
the OLD CURIOSITY CAT

Raise your hat to the late Reg Cat —
Lying there thinking "Well, that's that."

Shakespeare's Cat was a Ginger TOM
Nobody knows where he came from.
Illyria, Verona, Elsinore?
He may well have popped in from next door.
He finally died when extremely OLD –
The BARD thus inspired wrote "Poor Tom's a-cold."

When you're hailed as an Example of the *Taxidermist's* Art
Forget your Life's Ambitions —
It's now far too late to start.

IF EDGAR RICE BURROUGHS HAD HAD ANY SENSE
AND HIS PUBLISHERS
HADN'T BEEN PRATS
THEY COULD HAVE COME
UP WITH THIS AMAZING
IDEA
TARZAN - LORD
OF THE CATS

ULULATING CATS

Your pet-lovers are a peculiar breed
You can feed them on fish parts or chicken heads or seed

ZODIAC

ARIES believe in Fairies & savaging your Guests	**LIBRANS** like to weigh the Issue - DON'T ask for a Decision
TAUREANS are Conservatives as their name suggests	**SCORPIOS** can kill you with Immaculate Precision
GEMINIS are SCHIZOID & always in two minds	**SAGITTARIUS** - the ARCHER - NEVER call him Jeff
CANCERIANS walk sideways and become entangled in the Blinds	**CAPRICORNS** are blessed with horns - and play 'JERUSALEM' in F
LEOS love a PINT of BITTER	**AQUARIANS** are Water-bearers - and enjoy it in their Gin
VIRGOS hoe their used Cat Litter	**PISCES** are Fish & live in water - and do disgusting things therein.

But for the vertigo I could have been another Michaelangelo. As it is people still ask, as they will of Renaissance men, which job I like doing best and I always say 'Drawing' and explain that I must like drawing best as it's the only job I do during which I never look at my watch.

Ask me which drawing I like doing best and I would reply without hesitation 'The monthly cover for the <u>Literary Review</u>, arguably the World's Greatest Magazine'. The Editor, Auberon Waugh, and I have been together now for

forty years in _Private Eye_ and the _Daily Telegraph_ but it's _Literary Review_ covers that I enjoy most. Bags of room and colour, and always a cat somewhere in the picture, a tradition that started in May 1987 with this study of the Venerable A. N. Wilson _(left)_ in feline guise. In fact I think that since then only one cover has been catless and that had a goat on it, which I claimed was a cat in disguise. Sometimes, as in this tasteful study of the Poet Larkin _(above)_, cats abound.

In others, for example this family portrait of the Windsors drawn at the beginning of the <u>Annus Horribilis</u>, you have to search a little. And there it is, highly adjacent to the Duchess of York's celebrated toes.
(<u>Artist's Note</u>: I shall stick to cats. Quite clearly I can't draw Corgis. And I'm none too fond of the horse).

Now this one I'm very fond of. It celebrates the 400th Anniversary of Christopher Marlowe's still unsolved murder in Deptford. The fact that one of the suspects was called Ingrams allowed us to portray the former Editor of the Eye and now Editor of *The Oldie*, the eponymous Richard. The cat is quite easily spotted but none the worse for that.

Back to a host of cats, including I'm sad to say, a dead one, I hope no children are looking. This is the famous Wallace Arnold, less well-known as writer Craig Brown enjoying Venezia and its facilities.

I remember I was going to paint the sky grey and make the weather disgusting simply in order that I could insert the elfin joke 'It's raining cats and Doges' but Venice deserves better than that, a city of which I have only the happiest memories, so the sky went blue.

Lady Antonia Pinter wrote a book about the wives of Bluff King Hal and here is the Literary Review cover that resulted. Lady Pinter is rather unflatteringly portrayed in the background. I'm afraid I drew her from memory. Not, I hasten to add, that I have memories of her as such, but I had drawn her previously not unsuccessfully and thought I could do it again. Too late. Sorry.

Finally Northern Ireland. Not an easy subject. I've made the cat neutral I see by colouring one eye green and one eye orange. I'm not suggesting this as any solution to the Troubles.